You Are Precious To Me

Neeta Sahay

First Published in January 2020

ISBN: 978-93-89888-05-8

BLUEROSE PUBLISHERS
www.bluerosepublishers.com
info@bluerosepublishers.com
+91 8882 898 898

Cover Design:
Tyngshain Pariat

Typographic Design:
Teena Maurya

Distributed by: BlueRose, Amazon, Flipkart, Shopclues

Acknowledgement

I am thankful to all the persons who always encouraged me in my life and only due to their support it is possible to get this book published. I'm also thankful to the people who always discouraged me by passing on sarcastic comments and giving adverse remarks about my every small act, which gave me all the more grit and determination to bring this book in the world.

This book, the first venture of my life, has all the experiences of one's life– joys, sorrows, pleasures, pains, angers, depression, lighter moments, heavy moments and all. Please read all the poems of the book, and you may find in them depiction of your own feelings. It's the mirror of yourself, myself and the people around ourselves. There is a whole world hidden inside you, which, time and again, strives to come out to see the outer world. Yes, it's the world of literature out there, always expanding, never ending, very deep, just like an ocean, very high, just like the Himalayas. This book, "You're Precious To Me" is really precious to me, as it's my first baby. It's just like a drop in the ocean lost somewhere, yet striving for survival and get noticed by the intellectual people like you.

But first I have my duty to give acknowledgement to the people who really mean to me. Right from the beginning of my life my brother, Rajiva Bhushan Sahay, and my parents were always supportive to me. Bhaiya has been constantly a source of inspiration and helpful without whom I would not have ventured in the ocean of English literature. He always stood by my side in every situation.

My sisters Baby (Mrs Nina Rattanmani) and Rina Di (Mrs Rina Swarup), my cousins, always stood with me. While I was absorbed in writing and editing my articles, it was Baby who took care of my food and my rest. She gave me cups of tea and coffee whenever I felt drowning in sleep.

I will always remain thankful and cannot forget in my life, The BlueRose Publishers, which, without knowing me, gave me a chance to get my books published. Aman, Sugata Das, Bhanupriya, Tyngshain Pariat (Joel), Teena, to name a few, became my very closed friends, in the process of compiling, editing, designing and completing the books. BlueRose– a very good platform for the first time writer like me– has a very special place in my heart.

Last but not the least I am very grateful and obliged to my husband, Ashok Kumar Srivastava, who let me do whatever I wanted to do and never restricted me. He gave me wings and left me free in a big wide sky to fly. He always understood my feelings and did things accordingiy. Whenever I threw tantrums, he coped with me, sometimes doing the things against his will just to make me happy.

Thanks to all the members of my extended family who motivated me right from the beginning.

The title of the book. You Are Precious To Me is concerned with my parents to whom I dedicate this book.

Contents

Acknowledgement / iii

1. Pains / 1
2. Rememberance / 5
3. Separation / 6
4. A Single Girl / 8
5. The Young Teacher / 10
6. My Asset / 11
7. Death-A Blessing In Disguise / 12
8. The Nature In Pain / 13
9. What A Change! / 15
10. Money is not everything in our life / 17
11. The New Teacher / 18
12. O ! November / 19
13. Monday Morning Blue / 21
14. My Father / 22
15. First Love / 24
16. Emotional Bank / 26

Pains

Sinking very slowly inch by inch,
Now it's dawning on my brain,
She will never, never come to me,
I cannot see her smiling face again.

As I sat beside her dying bed, sensing
A noble soul struggling to quit a weak shell
She was at war with cruel death,
The equipments' beeps counting her breath.

Each new breath got weaker and weaker
Till the jaws of death became her soul seeker.
Previously I thought she would come some day,
She might have been to my Mama's place.
Sometimes I opened door s for her,
Thinking I heard her voice and her steps.

But finding no one became hopeless again
I saw not even apparition of her frame.

It never came to my simple mind
That people never return after they died.
Though I'm educated, they say highly qualified.
I still felt she'd come to be at my side.

The memory of her last breath
Still haunts my mind.
The spasms of her upper lip
Again and again,
The beeping sounds of medic instruments,
Which I couldn't all comprehend.

But somehow I knew they were
Signalling dangerous waves.
The bubbling oxygen in a glass container
told she was breathing under pressure.

The fragile thread between life and death
The doctor told she is in her last stage
We were informed in a hushing tone,
That she was going to be no more.

Still I couldn't take it seriously
As my father was reading 'Hanuman Bahu'
Hoping against all hope

It was a big joke of my life
I didn't lose my cool and strife.
I called her 'Ma', she replied in spasm,
Her opened eyes fixedly looking at Dad.

Suddenly it appeared the thread snapped
The nurses removed the equipments attached

I couldn't bring myself to cry
As there is no drama in life.
We're mentally prepared for her death.

But still couldn›t console ourselves.
Now a white sheet covered her face.
At that moment I was thinking of Shakespeare's lines
"Come away, come away death".
As an English teacher I recall all the elegies,
Written on cruelty of death.

When I came to my senses
I realized it was the hospital corridor,
Now her corpse was mentioned as body.
And one more life is no more.

Someone consoled us saying
"She doesn't have to bear
pains and sufferings any more."
She left her body and memories
For us to suffer silently.

When I returned after her funeral,
I found myself surrounded with
Lots of scandalous talks and rumours.
When I needed support and sympathy
They spread gossips and showed apathy.

I became an isolated island
With sea of sorrows all around,
There's no bridge to reach
I felt I was losing all the ground .

I've a void in my life now, sometimes
I was just on the verge of breaking down.
I'm already broken from inside,
I'm going to crumble down
It's only the matter of time.

P.S.
If I don't find any shoulder to cry my heart out
There's certainly going to be a
One more case with schizophrenic shout.

Rememberance

The red sindoor between her hair parting
The printed aanchal of her saree,
A round bindi on her forehead wide,
The yellow silk with border wide.

She used to work night and day
But never complained of her anginal pain.
She made for me Nimki and Khajoor,
Despite doctors' advice not to take strain.

Sometimes she used to look outside the window
Counting the buffaloes grazing in the meadow.
She was never harsh to anyone around,
Only scolded us sometimes to maintain the house.

When I felt sick, she became worried,
And used to bring me milk when I studied.
She woke me up every morning,
Reminding of my school-bus timing.

When I came back home tired and drawn,
She gave me tea with Choora-Badam.
When I created scene throwing tantrums,
Who else but only Ma'd bear such fussy daughter.

Separation

So many obstacles are there between them
Which stop the couples meeting each other.
Busy schedules and long distance
Traffic jam and job demands
Different cities or different brands
Phone not working, or ego problem
The causes of separation, to name a few.

Her constant wait and pining for him
Her efforts to seduce and cooking for him
Oh! How silly of her to try these things,
Knowing well these vain things will not melt him.
His hard-heartedness and dry romanticism
His practical approach, quite contrary to her emotions,
Her few loving lines of her sentimental mind
Not enough to move him or his mind.
She tries to become smart so that they can match.

Sometimes she tries to become homely
So that he doesn't leave her lonely.
She goes to parlour, and lure him to bed,
Sometimes she clads herself all in red.

She talks sexy things to attract his attention
She wants to cuddle in his arms to wipe out all tension.

She wants to live the life to the fullest
For her quality time with him is important
There is a whole life in a single moment,
She comes close to him to steal the moment
To tell him to enjoy every moment
Otherwise there is no return of the same moment.

A Single Girl

Wherever she goes, whenever she is alone
People pose the awkward question to show
That she is in fault to live her life
With her head held high,
They ask why she is still unmarried
At this stage of life? Why?

Everytime when she is faced with this querry
Her honour is on stake, she cannot make any merry.
They weave juicy stories all about her
Hearing these gossips she loses her composure.
There are vulgar looks when she moves out.
When she talks with her young colleague
She is all the more under doubt.

She is not safe in her single state
She is in trauma leaving her date.
Oh! Don't ask questions to make her irritate
Let us leave her alone to fight with her fate.
Her qualifications are her disqualification
She gets curse instead of commendation.
She is efficient in her duty
But they talk about her beauty.
They look at her smart colourful dresses

But don't see in her eyes the sorrows and distresses.
Why is she blamed for her single status!
As if she is a culprit charged with murder

People rejoice when she is sad and worried,
They pass sarcastic comments when she is hurried.
She is decried despite her education,
She is on her own feet but doesn't get appreciation.

Please don't break her heart, let her take breath,
She is already broken from inside
She will crumble down, it's only the matter of time.

The Young Teacher

Boys whisper, girls giggle,
Feeling attracted towards her,
But the colleagues talk behind her back Feeling quite jealous of her.

She is a young teacher, pretty and fresh Girls of her class comment to see her dress.
She is just out from college,
Smart and full of knowledge.
Amiable to girls, friendly with boys
There is no wide gap between their age.

They are enchanted, with her lesson,
Different methods to explain Narration
The English grammar which was boring,
Now the students find it quite absorbing.

Punctual and active, hard-working and strong,
But the Principal found in her everything wrong.
As she is getting popular response,
Her efficiency became a negative point.

My Asset

Don't snatch from me my pain,
This is my only asset to gain.
Whether you call me sane or insane
I just wish my mind to retain my pain.

Take away my money, take all ornaments
In my life they are simply vain,
I wish to abdicate all my reign
You're free to say I've no brain.

As long as I've paper and pen
I won't become insane,
They can help me to remain
Cool, and not to lose my brain.

The more intense my pain,
The more depth acquire my pen,
The sharper become my words,
The more I get good name.

Death-A Blessing In Disguise

They say to doctors,
please save me from death.
But I have to request them–
To save me from life.

Death is life, and life a death for me.
O life, could you please embrace me
To save me from death.
O death! You are not a foe, but my friend,
Come and spread your arms to hold me.

You give solace just like a Knight,
I am a distressed damsel in a prison of life,
Come to rescue me from the demonic life.
Give me blessing and give me a new life.

When you take away my life,
I will leave my body and all the worries of life.
Leaving behind my worldly love-life,
I trust you'll be my life-long partner,
And not a part-time lover just to pass time.
You can be a blessing in disguise to accommodate me whole life.
Amen...

The Nature In Pain

Wasn't the earth beautiful
With all its flowers and blooms!
The rivers flowing through the mountains
The bees humming their lovely croons.

The rainbow with its seven colours
A delight to the eyes.
The tiger with his ferocious fright,
And deer with its stride.
The birds twittering with their full might,
The peacocks dancing with delight,

The firefly showing its twinkling light
And giraffe proud of its height
Mango with its sweet flavour,
And stars in the sky.
Fish in a graceful swim,
Saving itself from the stork white,
The roaring lion, the king of jungle
Walking around in pride.

But now the rivers are polluted,
The fishes are becoming ill.
The trees are being cut and
Birds are becoming extinct,

Water is becoming unclean
Not to be drunk.
Chirping sounds are lost now
As the trees are getting hurt.

But who is responsible for the disaster
Who is to be blamed.
Who else but the vicious foul,
The mightiest of all,
Who calls himself human being,
But in truth the most devilish of all.

What A Change!

Previously we used to repel mouse
From our house,
Now we've a pad to place the mouse.
Once we wrote an application to be wise,
Now we use an application in our device.

An apple a day used to keep doctors away
Now in a digital world apple has its way.
The tooth never used to be blue,
But now it has become blue,
Why it is so, I've no clue.

Birds never got angry, on different sites,
Now they always become angry, and twitter too.
We used to read books and talked face to face
Now it's very common thing to read on Facebook.
Virus caused diseases when it spread
Now the words are spread to become viral.
The windows were fixed on the wall
Through which we used to look all.

Now the screen is windows, and
The Google became a portable ensychlopedia for all.
We made a sad good bye to our
Old fashioned, but faithful Kodak

'Cause no body can wait long to get photo.
Wow! What a change in the digital world
Man is going now beyond the Lunar,Neptune and Planetary world.

Money is not everything in our life

With money you can buy a bed,
But not sleep.
Money can buy a time piece,
But not time and peace.
It can buy a book,
But not knowledge.
It can buy medicine,
But not health.
It can buy a beautiful sculpture,
But not culture.
It can buy blood,
But not life.
It can buy red roses,
But not the nature's natural fragrance.
It can buy a house,
But it's up to you make it a home.

The New Teacher

She is a fantasy for school students,
They are spellbound with her ways.
Boys like her style and dressing sense,
Girls– struck with her earrings and lens.

Where does she come from, where does she go,
What does she eat and where is her home!?
Who is that man who sometimes reaches her school?
These pressing questions snatch their cool.

She is a mysterious inspiration for all,
Whenever she arrives to teach in the class.
The girls whisper(God knows what)!
The boys make signs behind her back.

When she explains them figures of speech,
They are bewitched with her
slender figure and voice sweet.
Her light aura, her straight hair,
Bring a fresh whiff of air.
Breaking the monotony of class,
She became a role model for all.

O ! November

O ! November, sweet November !
Younger sister of December.
Neither hot, nor too cold
You're as cool as cucumber.

The nip in the air, give you vigour.
Marigold, Lily, Rose, Lavenders,
Blooming flowers swing in the air.
Delight the gardeners' all green fingers.

Vegetables are plenty, eating a pleasure,
Cheese, popcorns, pizza and burger.
Apples, tomatoes, creamy crackers,
They get crazy with peanuts 'n' gingers.

With your arrival, the autumn is over,
Days are shorter, while nights get longer.
Summer gone for 5-months slumber.
All is well with the sunny splendour.

The glorious morning has a soft sweet flavour,
In the pink afternoon, the sun is softer.
Boys play as if they're Sachin Tendulkar, but alas!
It's getting dark, they can't play longer.

Girls wear their colourful sweater, with
Tunics, tweeds and matching muffler.
Some of them have quite an attitude,
Dancing 'n' holding on hot coffee tumbler.

Hurrah! Yippee, tra, la, la, la,
Twang-twang sounds good to ears, whether it's summer or winter season,
I like best the month of November.

Alas, you can't stay here forever,
You've to make way for December,
The time is flowing just like a river,
Never stopping, or resting ever,
Though never ever losing its vigour.

O ! November, sweet November !
Younger sister of December.

Monday Morning Blue

Oh, again it's Monday morning blue,
Why weekends end so soon, I've no clue.
It comes every week, like an uninvited guest
To spoil our tranquility and snatch our rest..

Why does Sunday not prolong longer,
To catch our sleep and enjoy longer.

Come on, sleepy head, it's time to start,
Get up quickly, take your bath.
Leave your bed, don't snooze your alarm.
Jogging can be skipped up,
But don't skip your breakfast.

Don't waste your time in your mobile,
Be ready to keep up your high profile,
Dress up smartly, arrange your file,
Tighten your shoes to walk an extra mile.

Save fuel, don't pull out your car,
Rather use the carpool, it's no harm.
A new day begins, let this day embrace you,
Smile and greet the sun, to erase your woe,
Freshen up your make-up to look your cool,
And say 'Bye' to Monday Morning Blue.

My Father

I'm a daughter of a good father,
Who supported us in every possible way,
Though his earnings were not much,
But we got enough butter and bread.

He loved and pampered me
And called me his princess precious..
When I cried he got sad,
At my smile he was glad.

He had an immense knowledge,
He was the prefect in his college.
He was honest and true to his words,
KeepIng away from vanlty.

Reading books in leisure,
Gave him much pleasure,
As the body needs food,
Reading was his mental nutrition.

I inherited a sense of right and wrong from him,
He valued ethics without preaching
He took me to the world of books
Inculcating in me the habit of reading.

As I was mediocre in Mathematics,
It was beyond my comprehension,
He taught me ratio, cube and fraction, L.C.M.,H.C.F.
etc. became to me easier.

He had a great faith in God,
And was always content whatever he got
Memories are still so fresh
As if it happened just yesterday.

When he breathed his last,
My world fell apart,
Leaving behind his legacy,
But leaving me blank.

First Love

It must be his first love,
He is just growing up.
Not yet attaining teenage
But started writing on blank page
The name of his first love,
The name of his first love.

The attraction between them
Growing up, growing up.
No matter, if, soon it will be
Blowing up, blowing up.

Her name is on his lips
When he is alone,
Imagining what she must be doing
When she is alone.
The first love is unforgettable
Remaining in the mind very stable.
Age or rank is beyond his thoughts
He thinks now he won›t wear shorts,
Instead, he will be in his trousers
To look senior and much maturer.

The growing boy has a growing desire,
In his fantasy he has the title of Esquire,

He'd happily leave for her his big empire,
If her father Lord Ullin stops his daughter
How silly of him to be a lovelorn creature
He's secretly languishing for her teacher.

She's lovable to one and all as a teacher.
He envies if anyone talks of her features.
She feels embarrassed when he stares,
The grapevine has report she's in affairsl

She's in dilemma about the man in her life
As these boys are uppermost in her mind.
Although they are kids, and half her age,
But she senses an infatuation for her in them
Specially the one who draws her attention,
He is her blue-eyed boy,
Whom she likes to mention.
Intelligent, and with dreams in his eyes,
Different from others, wisdom his prize.
Wonderful things happen in silence,
But never she takes leave of her senses.
She's flattered with all their appreciation.

But how can it be in reality! She has a fiance,
The 'spark' will soon be doused with time
It's just a teenager's passing fancy.
Now she is waiting for the final bell to go
Her date is out there, whom she cannot forgo.

Emotional Bank

Emotional Bank Account?
Sounds strange?
But try to create it in your own way,
It is something
Which adds flavour to your life.
It is something that remains
After completing your assignment
And a sense of satisfaction.

It is something like completing your syllabus,
Forgetting the content by 'them'
But the gratitude, love and respect
They cherish and retain for you.

It is something that your students
Even after their campus days
Touch your feet whenever they meet.

Whether you are a professional,
Student or a housewife.
Doesn't matter if you are poor,
As it is opened by good behavior,
It can't be seen, but felt and experienced.
Your interest will grow
Your little deeds of kindness,

Your little words of love
And your little help to others
Are returned to you in double.
Kindness is returned in kindness,
And good words are returned in goodness.

An investment in emotional bank
Does not require money, but nice thoughts
Got it? Worth treading this path!
Right from now.

www.ingramcontent.com/pod-product-compliance
Ingram Content Group UK Ltd.
Pitfield, Milton Keynes, MK11 3LW, UK
UKHW040014200726
13854UKWH00001B/194